**They look alike and they dress alike,
but they sure don't think alike!**

"I know I have to share a bedroom, Beth, but I think I'm entitled to my own thoughts, at least!" Sara complained, climbing into bed. When she saw Beth's face redden, she relented a little. "Five kids in a family is freaky!" she muttered. "This isn't a family, it's a *mob,* and I get lost in it! Why wasn't I born an only child, like Amy or Karen?"

But then you wouldn't have a twin! Beth thought. She was stunned. She knew Amanda and Jeffrey got on Sara's nerves sometimes, but she'd never considered that having a twin did too.

Other books about the Fifth Grade Stars

Fifth Grade S·T·A·R·S
TWIN TROUBLE

By Susan Saunders

Bullseye Books · Alfred A. Knopf
New York

To Heidi and Jenny

DR. M. JERRY WEISS, Distinguished Service Professor of Communications at Jersey City State College, is the educational consultant for Bullseye Books. Currently chair of the International Reading Association President's Advisory Committee on Intellectual Freedom, he travels frequently to give workshops on the use of trade books in schools.

Library of Congress Cataloging-in-Publication Data
Saunders, Susan. Twin trouble / by Susan Saunders.
p. cm.—(Fifth grade Stars ; #4) A Bullseye book.
Summary: A new baby in the family compounds Sara's already shaky problem of identity as a twin in a growing family, and her town's 150th anniversary celebration further complicates things as her fifth-grade club competes with a rival club to win the most prizes.
ISBN 0-394-89606-8   [1. Identity—Fiction. 2. Twins—Fiction.
3. Clubs—Fiction. 4. Babies—Fiction.] I. Title.
II. Series. PZ7.S2577Tw 1989 [Fic]—dc19 88-19773

RL: 5.6

Manufactured in the United States of America
2 3 4 5 6 7 8 9 0

◄ 1 ►
Sara's Problem

"Star Movers, coming through!" Jan Bateman squeezed through the doorway of the Greenfield twins' new bedroom with an armful of clothes on hangers. "Where do you want these?"

"Uh . . . let's see. . . ." Beth Greenfield pushed bright-red curls out of her face and opened the small closet, which was already filled to bursting. "I don't know—just dump 'em on one of the beds for now."

Beth and her twin, Sara, were moving downstairs in their two-story house, and Jan, Karen Fisher, and Amy Danner were helping them. Best friends, the five girls were the founding—and only—members of a fifth-grade club, the Stars.

Jan laid the clothes down and studied the room doubtfully, tugging at her brown bangs. Two beds, two chests of drawers, a desk, a bookcase. Beth's poster of a bunch of zebras and elephants sharing an African water hole with a lion, Sara's poster of a crumbling castle in Scotland, Beth's framed beetle collection, Sara's glass figurines. A cardboard box full of the grooming equipment Beth used on the cats and dogs, a huge paisley scrapbook of Sara's with pictures of places she'd like to live. Add to that enough clothes for two ten-year-old girls, a radio, and cassette players, tapes, stuffed animals. . . .

"Do you think you'll be able to fit everything in here?" Jan asked at last.

"Of course they will." Karen Fisher was sitting on the floor in the corner, carefully arranging Sara's figurines on the shelves Mr. Greenfield had made for them. Karen was tall and slender, with silky blond hair that was never out of place, and serious green eyes. "It's just a matter of being organized."

"I'm going to try really hard this time," Beth promised, cramming sweaters into one of the chests of drawers. Sara was the neat twin, so Beth knew exactly who Karen had in mind.

"Any room for a slightly freaked-out turtle?" Amy Danner was carrying the big glass terrarium where Beth's turtle, Herkie, lived when he wasn't swimming around in the bathtub. Herkie's head bobbed with every step Amy took. He had kind of a dazed expression on his green face.

Dazed—that's exactly how Sara's been looking, Beth thought. She frowned, a little worried about her sister. As far as Beth was concerned, the more that was happening—like moving downstairs, and the new baby coming, and getting the Stars' one-hundred-year-old clubhouse ready for the River Grove Sesquicentennial—the better she liked it. Beth thrived on excitement.

But Sara was different. She was quiet and shy and sort of daydreamy. She loved to read—she was even writing a book of her own. It was set in the days of castles and highwaymen, and described the life of a beautiful, red-headed orphan named

Tiffany Vandermere, and a dark, handsome stranger named Sean MacNeill.

Sara needed calm, and that was hard to come by in the Greenfield family. With each new baby, the Greenfields had moved: from the first small apartment on Post Street to a larger one on South Street when Amanda arrived, and then to Barton Lane to make room for Jeffrey. When Mr. Greenfield had heard about the subdivision going up on the edge of River Grove, he'd been very excited: "A big house, with plenty of space for everybody. Four bedrooms, a basement, a good-sized backyard—we can finally spread out!"

The family had visited the house as it was being built last spring. Sara hadn't minded that she'd be sharing a room with Beth, the way she always had, because their bedroom was large and sunny, with lots of windows. It overlooked the backyard, which ended in an old orchard, from the days when Sugar Tree Acres was a farm. "It's perfect!" Sara had said. "Our fourth, and hopefully last, bedroom."

Our family sure has a way of filling up its living space, Beth was thinking now as she folded sweaters, no matter how big it is. There's Dad's carpentry—it had started in the basement and overflowed into the rest of the house and sometimes the yard. And Mom's clippings—Mrs. Greenfield cut them out of piles of magazines and newspapers, articles about how to save time and money, or re-cover the living-room couch, or cook a twenty-pound turkey in two hours. And the pets—the dogs, Skippy and Emmaline; Beth's guinea pigs, George and Martha; the goldfish; Herkie, the turtle; two kittens; and Clementine, the Oldest Cat in the World. Then there's us, plus Amanda—she was seven—and Jeffrey—a noisy five-year-old . . . and the baby, due any minute.

The twins had only been living in their fourth bedroom a couple of months when their mother had told them she was expecting another baby. The baby would need a room close to its parents. Jeffrey couldn't move out of his room or Amanda out of hers—they were too young to live downstairs. That's why the twins were moving from their bedroom on the second floor into what used to be the first-floor den.

"At first, Dad and I thought we'd keep

the baby's crib in our bedroom. But since Sara's such a light sleeper and the den is a perfectly good room, we thought you might like to move down there, away from the racket," Mrs. Greenfield had said. "It's temporary, of course. Eventually, we'll add a room on for the baby, over the garage."

"It'll be great! We'll have the whole first floor to ourselves, just like having our own apartment!" Beth had said to Sara. "We're going to love it!"

"Would you please speak for yourself, just once?!" Sara had grumbled, which really wasn't fair, since the twins often answered for each other. "Dumb me—I thought we were finally settled. But we're *never* going to be settled!"

• • •

Beth had been hoping that with Jan and Amy and Karen helping with the move, Sara would snap out of her gloomy mood. But she could tell it wasn't working. The way Sara dragged into the room just then made Herkie the turtle seem positively lively.

Sara and Beth were identical twins. Both

of them had red curly hair, big golden freckles, and pale skin that blushed when they got upset or angry. Today Sara was looking paler than usual. Now she sighed distractedly and sank down onto a corner of a bed, a red notebook in one hand and her old stuffed unicorn in the other.

"Watch it, Sara!" Amy squawked. "You're mashing my foot!" She was kneeling on the bed, trying to slide Herkie's glass cage to the back of the desk, out of harm's way, and Sara had flopped down on her toes.

"Oh—sorry, Amy." Sara stood up again. "I didn't notice you."

"You're kidding!" Amy glanced in the mirror on the closet door to reassure herself. She was wearing an orange jumpsuit made of parachute cloth, and her hair was tied up with five neon-green pipe cleaners, which was what Amy called "creative dressing."

Sara didn't notice Amy? Beth thought. She's really in bad shape! "Sara, I know you've been feeling kind of out of it," Beth began.

"Who's feeling out of it?" said Sara. With a twin around I can't even have any privacy in my own head! she thought to herself. "I'm fine!" she added crossly.

"Could have fooled me!" Beth told her sister.

The twins so rarely bickered that Amy stopped adjusting her pipe cleaners to stare at them in surprise.

Jan spoke up before the argument went any further. "Let's listen to WPAX!" she suggested, quickly clicking on the radio.

"Hey! This is Lance Larson for WPAX, rockin' River Grove, 1012 on your dial, with a message from His Honor . . ." the deejay announced at the end of a song.

"Hello, folks, Mayor Bill Watkins here, to remind you about our exciting Sesquicentennial Celebration, coming up in a little less than two weeks. We've got a 'Gracious Homes' tour, the River Parade, the fair . . . and don't forget to buy your tickets to our beautiful pageant, 'One Hundred Fifty Years of River Grove'—the money will be used to . . ."

" 'One Hundred Fifty Years of Holly Hudnut' is more like it!" Amy leaned down to switch stations. "Since her mother's running the show, she's in almost every skit. I heard her blabbing to Brenda Wallace about it."

"Holly's been known to exaggerate if one of us is within earshot," Karen pointed out.

"Rrrgh! I can't stand that girl!" said Amy.

"Did you hear her buttering up Mrs. Campesi this afternoon?" added Beth. Mrs. Campesi was the River Grove Elementary School principal. "Holly makes me gag!"

" 'Oh, Mrs. Campesi!' " Amy shrieked, imitating Holly's piercing voice. " 'That's a *fab* sweater you're wearing! Mustard is my absolutely *favorite* color!' "

Even Sara giggled. Amy was getting better and better at doing Holly Hudnut.

"Even worse, Mrs. Campesi actually went for it!" Amy added. "Yuck!"

"You guys have to admit, Holly did us a big favor," said Jan.

"Like what?" Beth and Sara said at the same time.

"Without Holly and the Clovers, there probably wouldn't be any Stars," Jan said.

All five girls had been new to River Grove Elementary that September. Jan, Beth, and

Sara had come from different school districts, and Amy and Karen from different cities. Since they'd all moved into houses in Sugar Tree Acres, they had met for the first time at the bus stop, on the first day of school.

They had soon discovered they were in the same fifth-grade class, taught by Mr. Carson. It was in Mr. Carson's room that they had also discovered Holly Hudnut and the Clovers.

Holly Hudnut was the snobbiest girl at River Grove Elementary School. She was also the meanest and the sneakiest, but most people didn't see her that way. Most people—including the teachers, since Holly was superpolite to grown-ups and volunteered for everything—saw a dainty blond girl with big blue eyes, a turned-up nose, and expensive clothes, and thought she was practically perfect.

Holly *knew* she was perfect, and so did Brenda Wallace, Mary Rose Gallagher, Roxanne Sachs, and Sue Pinson. The five of them were members of the Clovers, although their club might just as well have been called the Holly Hudnut Admiration Society and Marching Band.

Holly was rich, and so was her second in command, Brenda. Brenda's house was as big as Holly's and modern, with lots of skylights and an L-shaped swimming pool. She even owned a horse, a registered Thoroughbred named Missy.

Brenda had a long face and big front teeth. She was more than a little horsey-looking herself. Mary Rose Gallagher, on the other hand, was attractive, and a good athlete. Mary Rose's family owned a house in town and a two-hundred-year-old farmhouse at their country place, where they kept *their* horse.

Roxanne Sachs was good at sports, like Mary Rose; but she'd recently become a lot more concerned about breaking a nail than making a basket. She spent all her allowance on makeup that her mother wouldn't let her wear. At the end of the school day, you could usually find Roxanne washing it off her face in the girls' room before going home.

Sue Pinson was a timid, mousy little

person, always wearing gray or brown. She was one of the best students in the fifth grade. She was also Brenda's cousin. Sue went along with everything Holly and Brenda said, and shared her homework with the other Clovers whenever they asked her to.

All the Clovers had side ponytails. They dressed alike too. If Holly wore a pleated skirt and penny loafers to school, so did the other four. They also talked alike and thought alike. It didn't take them long to come to a decision about the new girls: most definitely not Clovers material.

Of course, the twins and their friends had started out with a big strike against them—they rode the Sugar Tree Acres Route bus to school. Everyone else on their bus was a farm kid, which made the Clovers turn up their noses.

The Clovers had checked out Karen and Jan, though, before they had written them off completely. Karen was pretty, she was well dressed, and she was smart. . . . But the Clovers already had Sue Pinson when they needed *smart*. Maybe a club with two brains wouldn't be cool. On top of that, both of Karen's parents were scientists, working at weird old Brookville Labs! "I'm afraid Karen Fisher is a weeb in the making," Holly had finally pronounced.

Jan's father was the coach at Crestview High, and her older brother, Richie, was a football star. There were always long articles about Richie in the *River Grove Courier*, with pictures of him throwing a pass on the forty-yard line and winning the game. Richie was hot, which made Jan interesting enough to be invited to Holly's birthday party. But Holly hadn't bothered to hide the fact that it was Richie who'd impressed her. So Jan had avoided the Clovers from that day on.

As for Beth and Sara, Brenda Wallace had taken one look at them and exclaimed, "Totally impossible—red hair, freckles, and *those clothes*—the Gruesome Twosome!"

Amy's creative dressing made the Clovers smirk. At first Amy had been hurt by the Clovers' attitude—she'd been one of the most popular girls at her old school. Then she had gotten furious. It was Amy who'd said, "We'll start a club of our own!"

Beth agreed with her. "Why should we

sit around like a bunch of rejects and let Holly dump on us?"

So the Stars were born. The Clovers couldn't believe it—another fifth-grade club?! When the Stars came up with a fancy clubhouse, too—a small stone house built over a hundred years ago by J. D. Ellison, one of River Grove's founders—the Clovers were outraged! The Clovers and the Stars had been sworn enemies ever since. Each club was determined to outdo the other.

"Remind me to give Holly a big hug the very next time we see her," Amy said, making a rude noise.

"How's it going girls?" Mrs. Greenfield peered in at the chaos from outside the door.

"Just great, Mom," Beth answered.

"We'll have it straightened up in no time," Karen told her.

"How much longer, Mrs. Greenfield," Amy asked, " 'til the baby's due?"

Mrs. Greenfield looked down at her large stomach and smiled. "Sometime in the next couple of weeks," she answered.

"Five kids!" Amy marveled—she was an only child herself. "Neat! Maybe it'll be born on the Sesquicentennial, and have the same birthday as River Grove."

"Have you picked a name?" Karen asked the twins' mother.

"Jeffrey wants G.I. Joe if it's a boy, and Amanda wants Barbie if it's a girl." Mrs. Greenfield laughed. "I think the rest of us are leaning toward James or Jessica."

Beth had noticed that Sara had loosened up a little while the Stars talked about Holly and the Clovers. But as soon as Amy had mentioned the baby, Sara had gloomed again.

I'm going to talk to her about it, Beth decided, as soon as we're alone. In the Greenfield household, that was usually only at bedtime.

So before they went to sleep that night, Beth said, "You're not just upset about changing rooms—it's the baby coming, too, isn't it, Sara?"

"I know I have to share a bedroom, Beth, but I think I'm entitled to my own thoughts, at least!" Sara complained, climbing into bed. When she saw Beth's face redden, she relented a little. "Five kids in a family is freaky!" she muttered. "This isn't a family, it's a *mob,* and I get lost in it! Why wasn't I born an only child, like Amy or Karen?"

But then you wouldn't have a twin! Beth thought. She was stunned. She knew Amanda and Jeffrey got on Sara's nerves sometimes, but she'd never considered that having a twin did too.

"One of the four . . . no, *five* Greenfield kids—half of the Greenfield twins. Sometimes I don't know *who* I am!" Sara exploded. "Why can't I be plain old Sara Greenfield for a change?"

◀ 2 ▶
Amy Speaks Up—
Again

"You adjust to new things more quickly than Sara," Mrs. Greenfield told Beth the next morning. "We have to give her some time to get used to the new room. And a larger family. I'm sure she didn't mean what she said about being twins, sweetie."

Beth wasn't so sure. The twins had always parted their hair on the left. That morning, Sara parted hers on the right, even though a cowlick made it stand straight up in back. And she waited until Beth had gotten dressed in a red sweatshirt and jeans to pick out a pale-green skirt and a print blouse.

When they climbed onto the Sugar Tree

Acres Route bus with the other kids, Sara sat by herself behind Mrs. Purvis, the driver, and started scribbling in her red notebook.

She's probably putting her heroine Tiffany on a desert island again, thousands of miles from nowhere, Beth thought. Just where *she'd* like to be herself.

"Is something wrong with Sara?" Karen asked Beth as they continued down the aisle.

"She says she's tired of being a twin," Beth murmured. "She wants to be plain old Sara Greenfield."

"It'd be kind of hard to think of her as *not* a twin," Jan said, "since the two of you look exactly alike."

"We could pretend she was in disguise," Karen said helpfully. "Like Alexandra Cole, who turned out to be a humanoid from Regulus. . . ." Karen was always reading science fiction, or mystery stories. It gave her a different outlook on life.

"Sssh—Matthew loves to eavesdrop," Amy warned.

A boy was sprawled across the backseat, singing loudly along with his Walkman.

"Ooo-eee-ooo-ah-ah. Ting-tang-walla-walla-bing-bang. . . ."

"Give it a rest, Matthew!" Amy nudged him with her toe and made a face.

Matthew Ellis was tall and gangly, with ears that stuck way out. He could have been mistaken for a nerd. But he hung around with Pete McBride, one of the cutest boys in fifth grade, and he knew more about rock music than practically anybody. Although Amy complained about him being a nosy neighbor—he lived across the street from her—Beth had a feeling she liked him.

Beth thought Matthew was okay. He'd helped out the Stars more than once. Besides, he and Pete McBride drove the Clovers crazy. What better recommendation was there than that?

"Hey, girls!" Matthew grinned up at them and pulled off his headphones.

"Ick! What did you do to your hand, Matthew?" Jan asked.

Matthew looked at the big black bruise under his thumbnail. "Clunked myself with a hammer. No big deal. Pete and I are knocking together a raft for the Sesquicentennial."

"Since when are you going to be in the River Parade?" Amy said.

"Since we heard about the prizes. Two hundred dollars' worth of albums from Goony Gus's, two ten-speeds from Al's Bikes, a year's worth of passes to the movies at the mall . . ."

The girls sat down as the bus lurched forward. "What's your theme?" Beth asked him.

"We haven't decided yet," said Matthew. "We thought we'd think of a way to make the raft *go* first, and . . . heh! heh! heh!"— he gave a fiendish laugh—"stockpile balloons."

"For decoration?" Karen wanted to know.

Jan shook her head. "At River Parades, besides trying to win prizes for Best Theme, or Most Unusual, or whatever," she explained, "you try to get everybody else as wet as you can. That's part of the fun."

"Right," said Matthew. "We're going to make hundreds of water balloons."

"Paddling around getting soaked?" Amy sniffed. "It sounds awful."

"You'd have to be there," Matthew said

with a pleased grin on his face. He was really looking forward to it.

"Grand Central Station!" Mrs. Purvis bellowed as the bus screeched to a stop in front of the school. "Everybody out!"

• • •

On Thursdays, the first class for Mr. Carson's fifth-graders was their weekly library hour. As soon as the bell had rung, they trooped down the hall to the River Grove Elementary School library. It was one big room, with tall shelves around the sides, a card catalog and five round tables in the middle. The librarian's desk was next to the door, with a fifty-gallon fish tank gurgling away beside it.

Beth was first inside. She stopped for a split second to look at the swordtails and mollies and tetras swimming unconcernedly around. Then she dashed to the table closest to the windows and slid into a seat. She arranged her notebook, pencil case, and library books on the two chairs on either side of her.

"Sorry, these are saved," she said to

Jimmy Culver, a boy from her class. "Karen. Over here!"

Karen stacked the library books she was returning on the table: *The Clock Struck Thirteen. Red Alert on Planet Antares. Supernova! What the Butler Didn't See.*

Amy was carrying a large shiny book called *Found Jewelry,* with a picture on the cover of a necklace of spray-painted nuts and bolts. "Any good recipes?" she asked Jan, who was returning three heavy cookbooks. Jan wanted to be a famous chef when she grew up, and she was always trying out new dishes.

Jan's answer was drowned out, however, by shrieks of excitement from a girl with a long, thin face, and brown hair in a side ponytail. It was Brenda Wallace, screeching at the top of her lungs, "Holly! You're in the *Courier!*"

Mary Rose Gallagher, Roxanne Sachs, and Sue Pinson were jumping up and down near Mrs. Lewis's desk, their side ponytails bouncing around, while Brenda held a copy of the River Grove newspaper toward Holly. There she was on the front page, under the heading "Sesquicentennial Diary."

"You look fabulous!" Sue squeaked as she stared at the newspaper.

Beth and Amy made retching sounds.

Holly gazed fondly at her printed image. "I usually like my left side better."

"Who did Holly bribe to get into the newspaper?" Amy asked Sara. She'd slipped into her seat just as Mrs. Lewis stepped through the door.

"It's a picture of Holly in her pageant costume," Sara whispered. Beth got noisier around the Clovers, but they made Sara want to disappear.

"Oh, Mrs. Lewis! We borrowed your paper for a second. I hope you don't mind," Holly said with her phoniest smile.

"It's a lovely photograph, dear." Mrs. Lewis beamed at her as Holly folded up the *Gazette* and handed it back. "Please settle down, children," the librarian said to the class, "and get your books ready to return."

The Clovers had taken their usual seats, at the table in the center of the room.

"As you already know, all the fourth-, fifth-, and sixth-graders at both the River Grove and the Village Elementary schools will be turning in papers next week entitled 'What River Grove Means to Me.' I have just learned that the papers will be read by a committee of teachers from both schools, and then by Mayor Watkins. The writer of the best paper will be made honorary mayor of River Grove for a day during the Sesquicentennial!" said Mrs. Lewis.

"The first thing I'd do as mayor of River Grove is declare school over for a year," Pete McBride announced. He and Matthew were sitting with a bunch of boys at the table next to Holly's.

"For a century," Matthew added.

"And outlaw the Clovers," Pete went on.

"Right—anybody with a side ponytail goes straight to jail," Matthew agreed, as all the guys cracked up.

Making sure her back was safely toward the librarian, Holly stuck out her tongue at the boys and crossed her eyes.

"Maybe you could try to freeze like that," Amy whispered loudly. "You'd definitely get your picture in the paper again. You might even make the television news: 'Medical wonder with side ponytail knocks 'em dead at pageant.'"

"Mrs. Lewis . . ." Brenda whined.

"That will do, Matthew Ellis . . . Peter McBride," Mrs. Lewis said sternly—she hadn't heard Amy. She fixed the boys with a disapproving eye. "Starting with the last table, bring your books to the card catalog."

The Stars stood up to return their old books and pick out new ones. Beth wandered over to the fish tank again, and Amy strolled after her. She took the copy of the *Courier* off Mrs. Lewis's desk and studied the picture of Holly.

Holly was wearing a very old-fashioned dress for her part in the pageant, with a skirt down to the ground, long sleeves, and a high ruffled neck. "Does she look ridiculous, or what?" Amy murmured to Beth loudly enough for the Clovers to hear.

Holly shot out of her seat and snatched the newspaper away. "You're jealous!"

"Jealous? Of you looking like Mother Goose?" Amy snickered. "Get real!"

"How do you think you're going to look on the house tour?" Holly shot back.

"The best!" Beth said. "Our clubhouse is in great shape."

"Not your house, dummy—your clothes."

Brenda pointed a finger at Amy's yellow suspenders. "Your long dress'll be dynamite with those."

"What long dress?" Jan had joined them.

"You have to wear the kind of clothes people were wearing when your house was built," Holly said smugly. "And that wasn't jumpsuits, or baggies with high-tops."

Amy glowered at her. "You're making that up, Holly Hudnut!"

"Isn't my mother on the Sesquicentennial Committee?" Holly said, smiling triumphantly. " 'Participants in the tour will wear clothes of the appropriate period.' It's in the program." She looked down at the photo of herself again, her head cocked to one side. "I think long dresses are *so* romantic. . . ." Holly sighed happily. "I can't wait to see myself on the video."

Beth hated to ask Holly anything, but she had to know. "What video?"

"The one they're putting in the time capsule, of course," replied Mary Rose.

Holly rolled her eyes at the Stars' blank expressions. "The Entertainment Committee is making a video of the highlights of the Celebration. Then they'll bury it next to the founders' statue on the courthouse lawn, to be opened a hundred and fifty years from now," she said. "Parts of the pageant will be on it, and the march up Main Street, and the fireworks, and winners of all the contests. . . ."

"And the house tour?" Jan asked her.

"I don't know why they'd want to video-tape a bunch of old wrecks," Holly answered crossly, which probably meant the Stars' clubhouse *would* be on the video.

Brenda tossed her side ponytail over her shoulder. "The Clovers will be—if you'll pardon the expression—*starring* in the video," she said with a smirk. "Our great-great-grandchildren will be seeing Holly in the pageant, and me and Mary Rose in the horse show, and all of us in the River Parade. . . ."

"We're bound to win two or three prizes with our entry," Holly said breezily. "My father hired an artist to design our raft for us, with costumes to match. It's going to be fabulous!"

"Oh, yeah?" Amy said. "Don't count your prizes until you see our boat!"

"Amy . . ." Jan murmured, and jabbed her with an elbow. But Amy was off and running: "We've got a fantastic theme, and"—remembering what Matthew had said about his raft—"and lots of water balloons."

"Water balloons!" Holly stuck her nose in the air. "How infantile!"

Beth backed Amy up. "It's not infantile. It's part of the fun, and everybody does it. Are your costumes drip-dry?" she added sweetly.

"Be careful, Holly. With all that water around, you could melt, like the Wicked Witch," Matthew warned as he walked back to his table. He had *The History of Rock 'n' Roll* under his arm.

One of Holly's little pink sneakers suddenly kicked out and knocked his chair aside just as he started to sit down. Matthew collapsed on the floor with a crash that made everyone jump.

"Wha-a-at . . . ?" Mrs. Lewis exclaimed.

"Matthew Ellis again," Brenda called out.

"Matthew, I won't have this kind of disruption in my library!" Mrs. Lewis said coldly. "Please present yourself to Mrs. Campesi at once!"

"But Mrs. Lewis . . ." Pete protested as Matthew scrambled to his feet.

"No arguments, Peter, unless you want to go with him," Mrs. Lewis said. "*Now*, Matthew!"

As Matthew shuffled out, his face a dark red, Holly and the Clovers exchanged satisfied glances.

"Holly could commit the perfect crime," Karen said when Jan and Amy and Beth sat down at their table again. "No adult would ever believe she'd done it. She reminds me of Leslie Mason in *The Poisoner's Art*, who got away with murder. Or maybe she's more like the creature with radioactive blood in *Invaders from Centaurus*, who fried everything she touched. . . ."

Sara barely looked up from her red notebook until Jan reported, "Amy told the Clovers that we're in the River Parade."

"Oh, Amy!" Sara groaned.

"You didn't!" said Karen. Karen wasn't

very good on the water. In fact, although she looked athletic, she wasn't very good at sports in general.

"When I hear the Clovers raving about something, I have to speak up for us, don't I?" Amy defended herself. "Sara, can I borrow a piece of paper out of your notebook? I want to keep track of who's doing what at the Celebration."

Sara tore out a page, and Amy used it to make two lists. The one on the left side of the page had the heading "Us," which meant the Stars. Under it Amy wrote "(1) House Tour (2) River Parade."

The list on the right had the heading "Them," meaning the Clovers. Under "Them," Amy wrote: "(1) Pageant (2) River Parade (3) Horse Show."

Amy held the lists up so that all the Stars could see them. "Even if we're in the River Parade, they're still ahead of us!"

"Amy, we don't know anything about making boats," Jan pointed out.

"I know how to build furniture, remember?" Amy's mom, who was divorced from Amy's father, had wanted her daughter to learn how to do things for herself. So Amy had taken classes in rock climbing, lamp wiring, wilderness survival, and even furniture building.

"I've made bookcases, benches, and tables," Amy said blithely. "What's a raft if it's not a table with no legs?"

◀ 3 ▶

The Stars Get Busy

The Stars decided that the best place to put together their raft would be the Greenfields' backyard. "Dad has lots of wood left over from his own projects that we can use," Beth volunteered. "And we won't have to worry about the mess, because it's plenty messy back there already. We won't be bothering anybody."

Except *me*, thought Sara. When Sara needed some time to herself, she'd sit in the old apple tree at the end of the yard. It had a low-slung branch that was very comfortable. The pale-green leaves offered privacy, and Sara had adopted it as her special, personal retreat.

So where did the raft builders start working on Saturday morning? Directly under Sara's branch!

"That way, our stuff won't get mixed up with your dad's stuff, okay?" Amy said to Beth. As the only experienced carpenter in the group, she had appointed herself foreman.

"Right," said Beth.

Typical! Sara muttered to herself. Beth says it's okay, and it's as though I don't even exist. But she didn't argue—she took the hammer Amy handed her.

"We'll use these four big fence posts for the framework." Amy studied Mr. Greenfield's pile of scrap lumber. "We'll bolt them together at the corners, and then we'll lay boards across the posts."

Following Amy's instructions, the girls sawed and drilled and hammered all morning. They stopped just long enough to gobble down some bologna sandwiches at lunchtime. By the middle of the afternoon, they'd built a raft about six feet square.

"Not bad!" Beth exclaimed. "We actually did it ourselves!"

"Nothing to it," said Amy. "Like a big coffee table, only easier—no legs."

"How will we make it go?" Jan asked. The only rule for the entries in the River Parade was that they had to be people-powered.

Amy shrugged. "Paddle it, I guess."

Karen stepped onto the raft and bounced up and down. "It seems solid enough," she said. "When can we try it out?"

"It would fit in the back of my dad's truck," said Jan. "I'll ask him to drive us to the river tomorrow afternoon and help us launch the raft."

"We have two or three paddles lying around the basement," Amy said. "I'll bring them."

"Let's take the tools inside and get something to drink," Beth suggested.

They were sitting at the Greenfields' kitchen table, trying to think of a theme for their raft, when the telephone rang.

Beth grabbed it. "Hello?"

"Hello—I'd like to speak to Beth or Sara Greenfield, please," said a high, piercing voice.

"This is Beth Greenfield. Who's this?"

"This is Mrs. Hudnut. Mrs. Howard Hudnut, Holly's mother."

"*Sure* it is, Matthew, you turkey!" The other girls had stopped talking to listen. "And I'm Mrs. Campesi, telling you to cut it out!"

"I beg your pardon?" The voice sounded about a hundred degrees chillier. "This is *not* anyone named Matthew, I can assure you!"

"This really is Mrs. Hudnut?" Beth said breathlessly. "Mrs. Hudnut!" she mouthed to her friends, pointing frantically at the phone.

"Yes, I'm calling about the pageant, 'One Hundred Fifty Years of River Grove.' "

"You're calling about the pageant . . ." Beth repeated for the others. "The one Holly's in?"

"That's right. There are parts in it for twin girls, about eight years old. We'd cast the Thompson twins . . ."

Beth nodded. The Thompson twins were in third grade at River Grove Elementary.

". . . but I'm afraid they've both come down with chicken pox. You and your sister are old for the parts . . . but we can't be particular at this late date," Mrs. Hudnut finished briskly. "You are identical, aren't you? That's essential."

Mrs. Hudnut has probably seen us around town at least twenty times, Beth thought. "Yes, we're identical," she replied.

"Fine. We'll be rehearsing Monday afternoon at four at the Municipal Auditorium. Will you be able to make it?"

"You want Sara and me to be in the pageant?" Beth said slowly for all to hear.

Amy, Jan, and Karen grinned and nodded.

"Isn't that what I've been telling you?" Mrs. Hudnut replied sharply.

"We'll be at the rehearsal on Monday, Mrs. Hudnut," Beth said.

"Way to go!" Amy exclaimed when Beth had hung up the phone. She pulled her Celebration lists out of the pocket of her jeans. Grabbing a pencil off the counter next to the phone, Amy added a line under "Us": "(3) Pageant."

"I'll bet this has ruined Holly's weekend," said Karen. "Sharing the stage with some Stars?"

"Her weekend? Her life!" Jan giggled. "And by special invitation from her own mother!"

Beth felt a twinge of guilt. She probably should have talked it over with Sara before she had accepted. But she'd done it for the Stars, hadn't she? She sneaked a look at her twin. From the expression on Sara's face, Holly's life wasn't the only one that was going to be ruined!

As soon as their three friends had left, Beth heard about it. "How could you?!" Sara yelled. "I can't think of anything worse than being on a stage, with an auditorium full of people staring at me. Did you forget the Christmas play?"

Beth and Sara had been angels in their first-grade Christmas play. Sara had had such bad stage fright that she'd actually thrown up in Act Two.

"That was four years ago. You were only six years old," said Beth. "And you had the flu."

"I decided then that I'd never step onto a stage again," Sara told her.

"Come on, Sara. We can handle this," Beth said soothingly. "The parts were written for eight-year-olds, so there probably isn't much to say. Besides, if you choke up, I'll talk for both of us."

"I'd really appreciate it if you'd *stop* talking for both of us!" Sara marched out of the kitchen and into their new bedroom next door. "I can't even sit in my tree because the stupid raft's in the way!" she muttered as she stamped back out again, wearing her jacket.

"*You* could have said something about not building the raft under your tree," Beth retorted. She was blamed if she did talk, and blamed if she didn't! "Where are you going?" she asked as Sara pulled open the front door.

"For a bike ride. Alone!" Sara closed the door behind her with such a bang that the dogs started barking, and Mrs. Greenfield called from upstairs, "Jack, is that you?"

Jack was Mr. Greenfield. He'd taken Jeffrey and Amanda with him to the grocery store.

"No, Mom," Beth called back. "I'm afraid that was Sara."

"Oh, dear," said Mrs. Greenfield.

◄ 4 ►

20,000 Leagues Under the Langley

When Sara came back an hour later, she was carrying a small paper bag from Denny's Discount. She didn't say anything to Beth about it. In fact, she didn't talk to Beth at all. She just stomped into their room and closed the door. At dinnertime, all Beth got out of her was, "Please pass the potatoes."

Jan called later to report that her dad would help them launch the raft, but Sara didn't comment when Beth told her the news. The silent treatment lasted through the night and into the next morning. Beth wasn't even sure if her sister would come along for the launching. When Mr. Bateman honked his horn early Sunday afternoon, however, Sara followed Beth and Mr. Greenfield outside.

Jan, Amy, and Karen were sitting in the front seat next to Jan's dad. They waved excitedly as he backed his truck as far up the Greenfields' driveway as he could.

"Hello, Henry," said Mr. Greenfield. "The girls really worked hard yesterday."

"So I hear," said Mr. Bateman. He was wearing a green-and-white cap with "Crestview Tigers" printed across the visor.

They all walked over to the old apple tree, and Mr. Bateman leaned down to pick up one end of the raft. "Mmmph!" he grunted as he lifted it off the ground. "This is a heavy one—I hope it floats."

The girls looked at one another. "All wood floats, doesn't it?" said Amy.

"Mmmm," said Mr. Greenfield guardedly as he heaved up the other end. "Ready, Henry?"

"Lead the way, Jack," said Mr. Bateman.

He and Mr. Greenfield lurched across the yard toward the truck, with the girls directing them.

"Look out for Jeffrey's sandbox, Mr. Bateman," Sara warned.

"Just let me pull this wagon out of the way," said Karen.

Both fathers were huffing and puffing by the time they'd made it to the truck. "Open the tailgate, Jan," Mr. Bateman wheezed. He and Mr. Greenfield slid the raft into the back, next to the paddles Amy had brought. It hung out over the tailgate.

"Whew!" said Mr. Bateman, fanning himself with his cap.

"I think I'd better come with you, Henry," Mr. Greenfield said, wiping his brow. "If the raft is heavy now, just wait until it soaks up some of that river water. It'll weigh a ton, and you'll never get it back in the truck by yourself."

"Well . . ." Mr. Bateman nodded. "You're probably right. I'm afraid we won't all fit, though."

"I'll take my car," said Mr. Greenfield. "Where's the launch site?"

"I think Topping Park would be the simplest. I can back all the way down to the water," replied Mr. Bateman.

"Sounds good," said Mr. Greenfield. "I'll

meet you there, as soon as I grab a few things."

"I'll sit with the raft, Dad," Jan told her father.

"I will, too," Beth said, climbing into the back of the truck after Jan.

"Hang on tight," Mr. Bateman warned.

Karen, Amy, and Sara got into the front with Jan's father, and he pulled slowly out of the driveway.

Mr. Bateman drove straight into town, and right down Main Street. Beth felt as though they were already part of the Sesquicentennial Parade. People on the sidewalks were staring at the raft, smiling and waving at them.

At the end of Main Street, Mr. Bateman took the right fork to the East River Road, which curved around to follow the eastern bank of the Langley River.

"Isn't Brenda Wallace's house somewhere around here?" Beth asked Jan, as they rolled past large houses with landscaped yards.

Jan nodded. "It's on the opposite bank, though."

Mr. Bateman slowed down to make another right turn into Topping Park, a strip of trees and picnic tables next to the water. There was a paved ramp down to the river, where people put in their boats. Mr. Bateman backed carefully down the ramp until his back wheels were almost touching the water. Then everyone jumped out of the truck.

"It's a perfect day to try out the raft," Amy said, studying the flat surface of the river with a practiced eye. "There's no wind and the water's absolutely still."

"That's encouraging," said Karen nervously. "I hope."

"What a pretty canoe," Jan said, pointing across the river toward the opposite bank.

The canoe was dark red with a yellow stripe, and three people were sitting in it. The two at either end were paddling slowly upstream. The passenger in the center was trailing a hand in the water.

"It looks so peaceful," Sara murmured.

Amy shaded her eyes to squint at the canoers. "Do you know who that is?" she exclaimed.

"Who?" The other Stars stared harder.

"Holly and the Clovers!" Amy practically shouted. "Mary Rose is paddling in the bow, Brenda's in the stern, and Holly's loafing in the middle, naturally. Can't you see the side ponytails?"

"You're right. I think that's Brenda's house behind those trees—the one with all the skylights," said Jan.

"They see us!" said Sara.

Brenda and Mary Rose had stopped paddling. All three Clovers were peering across the river as Mr. Greenfield drove up in his old station wagon.

"What if they come over here?" Beth said.

"Let 'em!" said Amy. "Then they'll realize that we can put together a raft as good as anything their hired artist comes up with."

Mr. Greenfield and Mr. Bateman were dragging the raft out of the back of the truck. They staggered a little under the weight, then dropped it into the river with a huge splash. The heavy raft disappeared under the water for a few seconds before it popped back up.

"It floats like a cork!" Amy crowed.

The Stars clapped loudly.

"Hang on to it, Henry," Mr. Greenfield said. "I brought some rope. . . ." He reached into his car for a piece of rope about eight feet long. He stuck one end of it through a knothole in a board and tied it tightly. "We don't want the raft to get away from us," he said to the girls. "Or you, either."

"It sits a little low in the water, doesn't it?" Mr. Bateman murmured to the twins' father. The top of the raft was only a couple of inches above the water line.

But when Amy yelled, "Here I go!" and jumped onto it, the raft held steady.

Sara was still watching the Clovers. Mary Rose and Brenda had turned the canoe around so that it was pointing at the Stars, and they were paddling like crazy. "They're headed this way," Sara warned the others.

"Maybe we should paddle out to meet them!" said her sister. Beth jumped on the raft too, and it sank a little in the water. "Come on, Jan."

Jan leaped on, but Karen lingered on the bank with Sara.

"Uh-oh!" said Mr. Bateman as the raft sank even lower. "Girls, I don't think this is going to work."

There was a great *gurgle* from under the raft, and several enormous bubbles of air burst in the water around it.

Brenda and Mary Rose were strong paddlers. They weren't more than ten yards away when the raft gurgled again, tipped sideways, and dumped Jan, Amy, and Beth into the Langley River!

The raft was only a few feet from the bank, so the water wasn't very deep. But it was freezing cold, and the three Stars were completely drenched. They floundered to their feet, sputtering and sneezing, to be greeted by gales of giggles from the Clovers, who were warm and dry in their fancy canoe.

"I'll bet I can guess your theme," Holly called out. "Twenty Thousand Leagues Under the Sea!"

"I'll show you twenty thousand leagues under the Langley!" Amy was more than ready to swim to the canoe and tip the Clovers over, but Mr. Bateman waded out and pulled her to shore.

Brenda and Mary Rose paddled smoothly away, hooting with laughter. The three dripping Stars huddled together on the bank, their teeth chattering, while Mr. Greenfield and Mr. Bateman dragged the raft onto dry land and heaved it into the truck.

Mr. Greenfield drove Amy, Karen, and the twins home. "Well, back to the old drawing board," said Amy from the front seat of the station wagon. The car heater was turned up as high as it would go, but the girls were still shivering in their wet clothes.

"Maybe we should consult with Matthew and Pete," Karen suggested.

Amy shook her head. "What do we need them for? The problem was, the wood was heavier on one side of the raft than the other. We'll add a fence post to the lighter side to even it up, right, Mr. Greenfield?"

"It might work. . . ." the twins' father answered cautiously, although Karen thought he sounded doubtful.

"I'm *sure* it will." Amy was supremely confident. "And we've thrown the Clovers off their guard—they'll think we've given up." She turned around to look at the twins—one wet, one dry—in the backseat. "We'll wipe those suckers off the map, in the River Parade *and* in the pageant. Tomorrow's the big day, guys—your first rehearsal."

Beth nodded, and Sara swallowed hard.

"You're going to be great! See you in the morning," Amy said as the twins' dad pulled up in front of the Danners' house. "Thanks, Mr. Greenfield." She trotted up the walk, still dripping.

The Greenfields dropped Karen off next. When they finally pulled into their own driveway, Beth dashed into the house to change out of her wet clothes. She was drying her hair when Sara walked into their new bedroom.

"Did you see that creep Holly, laughing her dumb head off?" Beth switched off the blow dryer. "We'll see how funny it is when she has to share the stage with us at the pageant!"

Sara spoke to her sister for the first time in twenty-four hours. "I can't do it," she said.

"Can't do what?" said Beth.

"Be in the pageant. Just thinking about it makes me stop breathing," Sara answered with a shudder.

"We said we would!" Beth told her.

"No—*you* said we would," Sara replied sharply.

"I did, and I'm sorry," said Beth. "But we can't let the Stars down now."

"There are things you can do that I can't, and the other way around . . . although I can't think of any right now that *I* can do and *you* can't. . . ." Sara's voice faded out, but she pulled herself together. "I want to help the Stars, but it has to be my way. We're separate people, Beth, not just one person with two heads and four arms and legs named 'Twins'!"

Beth had trouble falling asleep that night. If Sara didn't change her mind, how was she going to explain to Jan and Karen and, especially, Amy? She knew Sara couldn't sleep, either, because she was tossing and turning for what seemed like hours. Their parents had long since gone to bed, Herkie had stopped bumping against the sides of his cage, and the house was dark. Just as Beth was finally dozing off, she heard Sara get up. There was a rattling of paper. Then Sara crept out of the bedroom and up the stairs to the bathroom.

Beth lay awake, waiting for her to come back. Instead, she heard water rushing through the pipes overhead. Was Sara taking a shower in the middle of the night? She's definitely getting weirder and weirder, Beth thought.

Beth turned on the light. The paper bag from Denny's Discount was wadded up on Sara's bed, empty. She decided to sneak upstairs herself and check on her twin.

The shower was running in the second bathroom, down the hall from their parents' bedroom. Beth reached for the doorknob and tried to turn it. It was locked.

She tapped on the door. "Sara?" she called softly. "It's me."

The shower suddenly went off. "What do you want?" Sara murmured from the other side of the door.

"Are you okay? Let me in!" Beth hissed.

"I'm busy," Sara replied.

"Busy doing what? It's twelve thirty!" Beth said.

"Go to bed. I'll be down in a little while." Sara turned the shower back on.

Beth meant to stay awake until Sara came down, but she was too sleepy. Her eyes closed, and she had a complicated dream in which Sara turned into a person she couldn't recognize at all.

Beth woke up to the smell of coffee drifting in from the kitchen, and sunlight pouring through the window. "Sara? Time to get up," she said with a yawn. "It's seven o'clock."

When Sara didn't answer, Beth peered at the neighboring bed. Then she shrieked. Her twin was sitting up, rubbing her eyes. Only it wasn't her twin anymore. It was a girl with pale skin, big freckles . . . and *black* curly hair!

◄ 5 ►

Plain Old Sara Greenfield

"What in the world . . ." Mrs. Greenfield had rushed out of the kitchen to the twins' bedroom as soon as she heard Beth yell. "Sara!" she exclaimed when she saw her daughter. "What have you done to your hair?!"

"I *said* I didn't want to be in the pageant, but no one would listen," Sara said quietly but firmly. "Since Mrs. Hudnut needs identical twins, I decided to do something to change the 'identical' part." Her mother looked so horrified that Sara added, "It's only temporary, Mom. It's just a rinse."

"Then march right up to the bathroom

and wash it out, young lady!" said Mrs. Greenfield.

"Mom, I'm *not* going to be in the—" Sara began.

"I don't care about the pageant! If you don't hurry, you'll be late to school on top of everything else!" As Sara stamped up the stairs, Mrs. Greenfield added, "You girls!"

"*I* didn't do anything," Beth pointed out.

"If we'd paid better attention to Sara's feelings in the first place, this might not have happened," Mrs. Greenfield said with a sigh. "I'd better call Mrs. Hudnut and tell her to look for somebody else."

"Eeee!" Amanda was shrieking in the upstairs hall. "Sara's turned into a *witch!*"

"Leave your sister alone, Amanda!" Mrs. Greenfield ordered. "Get down here and eat your breakfast before it gets cold. You, too, Jeffrey Greenfield!" Jeffrey was making burping noises about Sara's hair, and Skippy started barking at the black-haired stranger.

Sara stayed in the bathroom so long that Beth had eaten and dressed for school before her twin came downstairs again. She was wearing her bathrobe and she had a large towel wrapped around her wet head.

"Well?" said Mrs. Greenfield. "Did it wash out?"

Slowly, Sara unwrapped the towel. "Some of it did," she said.

Beth gasped. "Sara!" she murmured. "Your hair's *green!*"

Sara's rinse had faded from a shiny blue-black to a dingy greenish-brown.

"I know," Sara said, miserable. "The rinse must have had some kind of strange reaction to the shampoo, or maybe to red hair. Now what am I supposed to do?"

"I can't let you stay home until your hair gets back to normal," her mother pointed out. "It could take weeks."

"I might as well get ready for school," Sara mumbled.

Mrs. Greenfield checked her watch. "Five minutes. I'll find you a scarf."

The twins had to race to the bus stop. Mrs. Purvis was just closing the doors to the bus as they both jumped on. Beth shot down the aisle toward her friends in the back as Mrs. Purvis stepped on the gas.

"You almost missed it!" said Jan.

"Where's Sara?" Karen asked.

Beth nodded toward the mysterious figure in a big checked scarf and dark glasses, hunched down in a seat near the door.

"What's she done up like that for?" Matthew Ellis asked from across the aisle.

"Matthew, do you have to know everything?" said Amy.

"What *is* she done up like that for?" Jan asked Beth in a lower voice.

"She dyed her hair black," Beth whispered. "Because she didn't want to be a twin in the pageant."

"Strike out!" Amy groaned. She took the list of Clovers and Stars out of her jacket and scratched out "(3) Pageant" under "Us."

"I think she looks kind of neat, like a spy or something," Matthew was saying. He stood up so he could see Sara better. "Hey, Sara!" he yelled. "Turn around!"

Sara practically disappeared under her seat, and Beth hissed, "Leave her alone, Matthew!"

"But you told Mrs. Hudnut you'd be in the pageant," Amy said to Beth. "Why'd you suddenly change your mind?"

"You don't get it, Amy. Sara never said *she*'d be in the pageant," Jan told her. "And from what you know of Sara, is it really her kind of thing?"

"I guess not," said Amy thoughtfully.

"Sara says no one ever pays any attention to her as a separate person." Beth felt really bad about it. "And I guess she's right."

"Boy, they're going to pay attention to her today!" Matthew predicted.

When Mrs. Purvis stopped the school bus in front of River Grove Elementary, Sara darted around the building to the side door.

"She doesn't want to walk past Mrs. Campesi's office, or the front desk," Beth said to the others as they hurried after her.

"Good thinking," said Jan.

"It's almost time for the bell. Maybe nobody'll have a chance to say anything rude to her," said Karen.

She was wrong. The Clovers were standing just inside the door to Mr. Carson's room. They couldn't wait to give the Stars a hard time about their raft, but Sara's strange get-up was an even better target.

"Who are *you* supposed to be?" said Mary Rose.

Sara scurried past the Clovers, but her scarf slipped off her head as she slid into her seat.

"Brown hair!" Brenda yelled before Sara could pull the scarf back on. "Or is it *green?!*"

"Hmmm . . ." Holly cocked her head to one side. "I think she's supposed to be one of the Munsters."

"And I thought *red* hair was bad with freckles," Brenda said.

"Big teeth and a side ponytail aren't so great, either," Amy snapped. "Unless you happen to be a lopsided horse!"

The bell rang before Brenda could think of an answer.

Their teacher, Mr. Carson, was a nice guy. He didn't mention the scarf, or ask Sara to go to the board all morning.

At lunch, however, Holly and the others pranced across the cafeteria to sit at the table right next to the Stars'.

"I know why her hair's that color," Holly announced loudly to the other Clovers.

"The river slimed it?" Brenda offered. Holly and Roxanne Sachs giggled.

"Listen, Brenda Wallace—" Amy began.

"Only *one* of them was in the river," Mary Rose interrupted. "Maybe the other one's smarter than she looks, although I . . ."

But Jan cut her off. "For your information, Brenda, Sara's dyed her hair as part of our theme for the River Parade!"

"From what I hear, you don't have a raft that works. Are you going to join hands and swim?" Roxanne snickered.

"All the raft needs is a minor adjustment," Karen replied coolly. "Finished, everybody? It's gotten stuffy in here."

The Stars stood up and marched stiffly out of the cafeteria.

"Thanks for sticking up for me," Sara said, tying her scarf tighter. "I know I let you guys down."

"We'll concentrate on the River Parade. That's something all of us can do together," Jan said.

"So you're not great in front of an audience. You're good at other things!" said Amy generously.

Like what? Beth could almost hear Sara thinking.

"We are going to be able to fix the raft, aren't we?" Karen was asking Amy.

"Sure," Amy said. "Absolutely. Another fence post on the lighter side, maybe a centerboard to steady it in the water if we need one. We might even think about a sail. We have almost two weeks to fine-tune it 'til it's just right. The Clovers will eat their words!"

•   •   •

The next afternoon after school, Jan convinced her brother, Richie, to drive the raft back to the Greenfields'. The girls quickly nailed on another post. Then Richie took the Stars and the raft to Topping Park.

"The new post will straighten it up," Amy said as the five girls pushed, and Richie pulled, at the now even heavier raft.

"I should have brought along the Tigers wrestling team," Richie panted. "Okay. On the count of three, really give it all you've got. One . . . two . . . three!"

The Stars shoved with all their might. Richie barely had time to get out of the way before the raft dropped out of the back of the Batemans' truck.

One end hit the ground with a thud. Then

the raft flipped over, smacking the surface of the Langley.

"Amy . . . ?" Sara said anxiously as the raft was swallowed up by the river.

"No sweat," Amy said. "It'll bob right back up."

Five seconds passed. Ten seconds. The girls crowded up to the water's edge.

"I don't even see it," Jan said.

"There it is!" Beth pointed to several trails of little bubbles. "I think it's stuck in the mud!"

Amy pulled off her high-tops and waded into the river. She groped around for the raft on the muddy bottom.

"Move over." Richie was strong—besides being on the high-school football and wrestling teams, he lifted weights every day. But even he couldn't budge the raft. "We'll drag it out with the truck," he decided.

"Why bother? It's never going to float now." For once, Amy was totally discouraged. "No pageant, no River Parade," she muttered. "All we've got to look forward to is standing around in long dresses at the clubhouse. Whoopee."

A large blue van turned off the East River Road into Topping Park.

"With our luck, it's the Clovers," Amy said glumly, "coming to gloat."

"Holly Hudnut in a van? No way," said Beth.

"That's the McBrides' van," said Richie. Pete McBride's mother taught biology at Crestview High. Richie was in her class.

"Yeah! It's Pete, and Matthew!" Beth said. The boys hung out the window to wave at them. "What are they doing here?"

Mrs. McBride turned the van around and edged toward the water. Pete and Matthew jumped out of the front seat as soon as she'd stopped. They raced around the van, threw open the double doors at the back, and stood aside. "Our raft!" they announced proudly. "Not bad, huh?"

"Wow!" Jan and Beth exclaimed.

The raft was made of a thick rectangle of plywood. It was big, it was light, and it was mounted on three air-filled rubber floats.

"Are floats allowed?" said Amy.

"Anything that works is allowed," Matthew answered. He and Pete lifted the raft out of the van and set it down on the water. It floated like a feather.

"It could probably hold eight or ten people!" Beth said. Like Pete and Matthew and the five Stars! But would the boys go for it? And what about Amy? She knew Amy preferred that the Stars do things on their own, but this was a great opportunity!

"How does it move?" Jan asked.

"That's the neat part," said Pete, jumping into the van.

"See the notches cut across the back, in the two wooden brackets?" said Matthew to the girls. "A paddle wheel fits in there."

When Pete emerged, he, Richie, Mrs. McBride, and Matthew dragged a huge wire wheel with wooden flaps attached out of the van. Then they slid the wheel onto a long, round dowel and fitted the dowel into the notches.

"It looks like the wheel in a hamster cage," Beth said.

"Yeah, and we're the hamsters," said Matthew. "One of us'll get inside the wheel and run."

"He means me," said Pete. "Matthew's too tall to fit."

"That turns the wheel, and makes the flaps slap the water, which'll push the raft forward," Matthew went on.

"Neat!" Beth exclaimed.

"Who thought of it?" Amy frowned, really sorry *she* hadn't.

"My dad," said Matthew. "The wheel was part of an old air-conditioning system at his office."

"Steering?" said Karen.

"We'll steer it with a paddle," Pete replied.

"We're adding a big wooden V to the front of the raft. We'll use long strips of inner tube to launch the balloons," Matthew said.

"So there's one of you running . . . and one of you steering . . ." Jan was thinking along the same lines as Beth.

"Right." The boys nodded.

"Then who's launching the balloons?" Beth asked, poking Amy with her toe.

"That's a problem," Matthew admitted. "We won't be able to blitz anybody while the raft's moving."

"You need a crew," Beth prompted them.

"Yeah. We asked my mom to steer," Pete said, "but she turned us down flat."

"I hate to get wet," Mrs. McBride told them.

"My dad can't do it, either, because he'll be helping out at the fair that day, and so will Matthew's," Pete said.

"My mom's no good. She can get sea-sick just looking at a picture of a boat," Matthew added.

"What about kids from school?" Jan said, with a meaningful glance at Amy.

"If we asked any of the guys, they'd want to share the prizes," said Pete. "We've done all the work. Why should we have to share?"

"Who said anything about guys? I'm short enough to run in the wheel, and probably Beth is, too." Amy gave in with a sigh.

"Jan's got great aim. She could help you with the balloons," Beth told the boys. She was careful not to volunteer Sara for any-thing.

"A boatload of girls?" Pete McBride said, doubtful.

"We'll decorate the raft for you," Karen said quickly.

"But the prizes—" said Matthew.

"We don't care about the prizes," Beth said.

"We just want to beat the Clovers," said Amy.

"We don't have a theme yet," Matthew said.

"Uh . . . what about 'Twenty Thousand Leagues Under the Sea'?" Beth had suddenly remembered the dig Holly made when the raft dumped the Stars in the river. It would really gripe her if we won something with her idea! Beth thought gleefully.

"We could have mermaids!" said Karen.

"And Davy Jones's locker," said Jan.

Matthew nodded. "Not bad. My dad's got a stuffed swordfish we could borrow."

Sara spoke up. "Jeffrey has a six-foot rubber shark."

Amy was looking more enthusiastic. "Some of us could dress like drowned pirates—wear lots of white makeup, and raggy clothes. I've got a great tie-dyed T-shirt with holes in it."

Before they could make any more plans, Jan's mom drove up in her car and tooted the horn.

"Hey, Mom!" Jan trotted over to the car. "We're going to be in the River Parade on Pete and Matthew's raft!" Then she spot-

· 68 ·

ted Jeffrey and Amanda Greenfield in the backseat.

"Beth—Sara!" Mrs. Bateman called to the twins.

"Guess what?" Jeffrey yelled.

"Mom went away in an ambulance," Amanda reported.

"Is everything okay?" Beth asked quickly.

Mrs. Bateman smiled. "Your mother's at the hospital, having her baby."

◀ 6 ▶
A Beautiful Baby

The baby was born that Tuesday night. The telephone rang at the Greenfields' just after midnight.

"We'll get it, Gran," Sara called up the stairs. Their grandmother was staying with the kids until after their mother came home.

Beth rushed to pick up the wall phone in the kitchen. "Hello?" she squeaked. "Daddy?"

"That's right, Bethie." Mr. Greenfield sounded tired but happy. "It's a girl, Jessica Elaine, six pounds, eight ounces. She's gorgeous, and your mother is just fine. Tell Grandma Keaton, okay? See you tomorrow."

"What is it?" Sara asked as soon as Beth had hung up the phone.

"A girl—Jessica Elaine Greenfield!" Beth answered. "And Daddy says she's gorgeous!"

"Daddy always says that," Sara pointed out. "He even said Jeffrey was gorgeous, and Jeffrey looked like a wrinkled-up monkey."

But this time Mr. Greenfield hadn't exaggerated. The twins saw the baby in the hospital nursery after school on Wednesday. Jessica Greenfield didn't look like a monkey, or like anybody in the family, either, not the red-headed twins, or brown-haired Jeffrey and Amanda, or their dark-haired parents. Jessica had lots of curly blond hair, enormous dark-blue eyes, and warm-pink skin.

"The only thing worse than *three* girls is *four* girls," muttered Jeffrey.

"She's the prettiest baby in the nursery," said Sara.

"She's neat!" said Beth.

"She'll do," Mr. Greenfield said proudly.

· · ·

"Nobody'll ever get Jessica mixed up with anyone," Sara said as she and Beth were doing their homework that evening.

"Sara, nobody who really knows you gets *you* mixed up with anyone, either," Beth told her. Especially not when you're wearing a scarf and dark glasses, she added to herself with a grin.

"I'm serious!" Sara said. "Sometimes I worry about being thought of only as a twin," she went on slowly. "But I think if I weren't a twin, no one would notice me at all. Jan and Amy and Karen are great about it, but I'm afraid the only reason I'm a Star is because of you. What do *I* do for the club?"

"You're nice, you're a good writer . . ." Beth began.

"See what I mean?" Sara said. "I'm not fun like Amy, or a good athlete like you and Jan, or as smart as Karen. I'm not anything."

Feeling sad, she picked up her pencil and wrote at the top of a piece of paper, "What River Grove Means to Me." Before she had filled half the page, her expression began to change.

Sara's the only person I know who cheers

up when she's working on a composition, Beth thought. Now she felt better, too.

That week there was the paper to finish and hand in, and Jessica's homecoming on Friday. The Stars had to come up with costumes for their entry in the River Parade, and they had to finish fixing up their clubhouse before the Celebration began, the following Wednesday.

All the schools in the area closed early that day. Before Mr. Carson dismissed his class at lunchtime, he made a short speech. "I very much enjoyed reading all the papers on what it means to you to live here in River Grove. One of the papers, however, was exceptional. I won't embarrass her by reading it aloud at this time, but I do want to say that I will be submitting Sara Greenfield's composition for publication in the *Courier*."

Sara ducked her scarfless head. After repeated shampooings her hair was copper with a greenish overlay, like an old penny.

"Congratulations, Sara—an excellent piece of work. That's all, class. Have a great time at the Celebration, and I'll see you next week."

"Hey, Sara!" Matthew said as they filed out of the room. "Maybe you'll get to be mayor!"

"I'm sure a sixth-grader will win," Sara answered shyly, but she looked pleased.

"You could appoint me and Matthew co-chiefs of police," Pete suggested. "We promise to clean up the town by getting rid of all of the Clovers. . . ."

"Chief Dog-Catcher would be more like it," Holly hissed. "Out of the way, clown." She gave Pete a shove as she stormed down the hall.

"Where's the fire, Cloners?" Matthew asked as the Clovers swept past in Holly's wake.

"Holly has to get ready for the pageant, bozo," snapped Brenda Wallace over her shoulder.

• • •

The Stars went to the pageant that afternoon with Mrs. Greenfield, Amanda, Jeffrey, and Jessica. Mr. Greenfield had wangled front-row seats in the Municipal Auditorium for all of them.

On the stage, Mayor Bill Watkins, wearing a false beard and a long tailcoat, welcomed "all River Grovers, old and new." He bowed toward Jessica's stroller when he said "new."

"Way to go, Jessica," Beth said, giving the stroller a jiggle.

"I want you to sit back, relax," Mayor Watkins went on, "and imagine yourselves back in time, before the middle of the last century. River Grove then was a ramshackle collection of wooden cabins, a church, and a general store, huddled on the bank of the Langley River. The citizens had just hired their first sheriff"—he pointed to himself—"that's me, Sheriff Melvin Hughes, to protect them against a band of cutthroat river outlaws led by Blackjack Wallace, the nastiest of them all."

"Wallace!" Amy exclaimed. "So Brenda comes from a long line of Terminators!"

"Sssh!" Mrs. Greenfield warned as the curtain went up.

The girls watched Mayor Watkins/Sheriff Hughes rub out the river outlaws in the first skit of the pageant. In the second, they saw Herbert L. Topping and J. D. Ellison, two of River Grove's founders, close down a gambling den and start the town's first bank.

"J. D. Ellison looks scary," Beth whispered, as a man with a black beard and a thick black mustache chopped down the door of a saloon with an ax. "I can't imagine him building our clubhouse."

"What about teaching our class?" Karen whispered back. "It's Mr. Carson! I recognize his nose."

Then the curtain rose for the third skit. "This must be the one about the big River Grove fire," said Jan. "See the livery stable in the background? That's where it started. It nearly burned down the town."

Twin girls in lace blouses and long gray skirts, with checked sunbonnets on their heads, sat on a park bench.

"The Thompson twins," Karen murmured to Sara. "Recovered from their chicken pox."

Amy gave a low whistle as Holly Hudnut sashayed out of the wings.

Holly was wearing a long pink-and-white dress with a huge skirt and lots of petticoats. Her blond hair hung down in large, loose curls. The curls bounced as she paused in the middle of the stage to give everyone a chance to admire her. Then she smiled her phoniest smile.

"What a ham!" Beth snorted.

"Do you realize we'd have been on stage with *her*?" Sara murmured. "Talk about gruesome!"

"She's sure wearing lots of makeup," Jan murmured.

"Probably Roxanne's," said Beth.

"No side ponytail, though," muttered Amy. "And I always thought that rubber band was holding her head on."

The Stars giggled, and even Mrs. Greenfield smiled.

Jessica Greenfield had slept soundly through the fake gunshots, shouting, and chopping noises coming from the stage above her. But as soon as Holly opened her mouth, Jessica started to whimper.

"I declare!" Holly screeched her lines in her piercing voice, fanning herself with one hand. "It must be a hundred degrees in the shade!"

Jessica's whimper turned into an unhappy wail.

"Oh, dear!" said Mrs. Greenfield, rolling the stroller back and forth to calm the baby down.

Holly moved closer to the front of the stage and sniffed the air two or three times. "Do you children smell smoke?" she shrieked at the Thompson twins.

At the sound of Holly's voice again, Jessica's wail became a full-fledged scream.

Holly frowned down at the Stars sitting in the front row. Beth and Amy grinned up at Holly and shrugged helplessly as Jessica's screams got louder and louder.

"I'd better take her out," Mrs. Greenfield said, standing up.

"You stay, Mom," said Sara. "I'll do it."

"I'll go, too," said Beth.

"So will I." Amy stood up as well.

Everyone except Mrs. Greenfield and Amanda trooped out of the auditorium. As soon as they stepped out the side door, with Jeffrey wheeling the stroller, Jessica stopped crying.

"I think she's okay now," said Sara. "I guess we can go sit down again."

"Are you kidding? Jessica stopped crying

because she can't hear Holly Hudnut anymore." Amy smiled approvingly at the baby. "Only eight days old, and already she's got great taste!"

Beth nodded in agreement. "Amy's right. If we take Jessica back inside, she'll start up again. We'd better hang around out here."

"Let's go to the fair!" said Jeffrey.

The exhibits, game booths, food stalls, and rides were spread out on the grounds in back of the Municipal Auditorium.

"We should wait for Mom," Sara said.

"The pageant'll last for a while," said her sister. "It wouldn't hurt if we walked around, as long as we got back before the show ended."

"Yeah. We could grab something to drink, and maybe a corn dog," Amy said.

So the Stars and Jeffrey hurried toward the fair, with Jeffrey pushing the stroller, and Jessica gurgling happily inside it.

Even louder than the five or six different kinds of music blaring from separate booths and rides was a loudspeaker making announcements: "Betty Carter, please meet your husband at booth number eight. . . .

The pie-eating contest starts in five minutes, in the tent next to the Ferris wheel. . . . Lost: one pair of dark glasses, green-wire frames. Please return them to . . ."

"Let's check out the pie-eating contest!" Amy said. "I heard Tucker McGill was going to try it." Tucker McGill was an eighth-grader who was already over six feet tall and weighed two hundred fifty pounds.

Wheeling the stroller, Jeffrey followed the Stars past a ring-toss booth, a wheel-of-fortune stand, and a round bumper-car rink.

"Found," the loudspeaker boomed, "a silver ID bracelet with the name Melanie on it. . . . The Pretty Baby Contest starts in fifteen minutes in front of the merry-go-round. . . . Don't forget to sample the great food at the Presbyterian Church tent. . . ."

"There it is!" said Beth. People were streaming into a small square tent next to the Ferris wheel, through a door with a sign above it reading PIE-EATING CONTEST TO BENEFIT THE ELKS—ADULTS 25¢, CHILDREN UNDER 12 FREE.

Inside, a long, low table stretched all the way across the tent, with folding chairs lined up on one side and at both ends. In each of the chairs sat a contestant, with nine pies spread out on the table in front of him.

"Look at Tucker," said Amy.

Tucker McGill was tying an enormous dish towel under his double chin, and arranging his nine pies neatly in three rows. "What happens when we run out?" he called to a judge. "Do you bring more?"

"You'll eat everybody under the table, Tuck!" one of his friends shouted.

The girls weren't so sure. There was an enormous man in overalls who looked as though he could eat nine pies, plates and all, in three seconds flat. Another contestant was bragging that he'd already scarfed down ten pancakes as an appetizer.

Suddenly Karen exclaimed, "Hey, there's Matthew!"

"You're kidding!" said Beth.

But it was Matthew, sitting near the end of the table, wearing his lucky shirt, the one with the red horseshoes on it.

"He wouldn't make a decent toothpick for these other guys!" said Amy. "The biggest thing about Matthew is his ears."

"Matthew, what are you doing here?" Jan asked after they'd pushed their way down to his end of the table.

"I got hungry," Mathew said with a shrug. "I figured this'd be a great place for some free grub." Matthew was a skinny guy, but he had a sizable appetite.

"We're starting the countdown," said a man holding a bell. "Are you ready?"

"Ready!" roared the contestants. Matthew grinned.

"No forks?" said Karen.

Matthew held up his hands and wiggled his fingers.

"Ten . . . nine . . . eight . . . seven . . . six . . . five . . . four . . . three . . . two . . . one"—*clang!* went the bell—"GO!"

Some of the eaters dug into their pies with their fingers, like Matthew. Others didn't bother with the niceties—they just picked up the pies and buried their faces in them.

"Gross!" Amy groaned.

"Faster, Matthew!" Jan urged.

"Tucker's already on his third," Beth reported. "Jeffrey, can you see?" she asked without looking away from Tucker McGill. "I can't believe how much he can stuff into his mouth without swallowing! He's finished with his third, and grabbing his fourth! Jeff, want me to lift you up on my shoulders?"

When Jeffrey didn't answer, Beth finally looked down. Jeffrey wasn't in front of her. He wasn't behind her . . . he was gone!

"Sara, where's Jeffrey?" Beth said as calmly as she could.

"Jeffrey?" Sara's face lost all its color. She gazed anxiously around at the crowd, but there was no sign of a little boy pushing a baby in a stroller.

The twins stared at each other, horror-struck. Now Beth turned so pale that her freckles faded.

Jan had stopped watching the contest. "Is something wrong?" she asked them.

"Jeffrey and Jessica have disappeared!" the twins said at the same time.

"What did you say?" Amy turned around, too.

"Jeffrey and Jessica—they're gone," Jan repeated.

Amy had been trained to handle sticky situations in wilderness survival, so she took charge. "The most important thing is, don't panic," she said firmly. "We'll find them."

"When was the last time you noticed Jeffrey?" Karen asked.

"Uh . . . when we came in here . . . or was it outside, near the Ferris wheel?" Suddenly Beth wasn't sure.

Sara looked ready to cry. "What'll we tell Mom?"

"Karen and I'll double-check the crowd in here," Jan said.

"We'll get started outside," said Amy. She headed for the door.

As soon as Matthew noticed there was trouble, he left his place at the table, wiping his blueberry-covered hands on his jeans. "I'll help you," he said.

As Tucker McGill crammed down his seventh pie and the crowd chanted "Tuck-er, Tuck-er," Matthew pushed his way to the door too. Beth and Sara were outside, totally frantic.

"Did you see a little boy with a blue

stroller leaving the tent?" Beth asked the man taking money.

He shook his head. "I'm not likely to notice one little boy, with all these people wandering in and out. Sorry."

Sara gazed hopelessly at the jumble of tents and rides and fair-goers. "It's so huge, and the kids are so small. How are we ever going to find them?" Her voice trembled.

"If I were Jeffrey's age," Amy said, "I'd probably be watching the bumper cars."

"You're right!" Beth dashed toward the bumper-car rink, and the others followed.

"There's a little boy standing next to the man in the green hat," Matthew called out.

"Not Jeffrey—too short," said Amy.

The four of them saw lots of little boys as they circled the rink, but none of them was pushing a blue stroller.

A wide walkway led from the back of the Municipal Auditorium to the big carousel, dividing the fairgrounds in half. "We'd better split up," Amy said. "Beth, you and Matthew look to the left of the walkway, Sara and I'll look to the right. We'll meet at the merry-go-round in fifteen minutes."

"What about Jan and Karen?" Beth asked.

"They'll catch up with us," Amy replied, grabbing Sara's arm and striding away.

• • •

Later Beth didn't know if it was the shortest fifteen minutes of her life, or the longest. It felt short because there were so many places to look—it would have taken all day to do it carefully. But when they didn't find Jeffrey and the baby right away, each minute that passed seemed like an hour.

"Maybe the livestock exhibit," Matthew said, pointing to a large blue-and-white tent. "Boys like pigs."

Beth and Matthew rushed past row after row of cages filled with fancy chickens and rabbits, and square stalls of cows, and pigs, and sheep. Jeffrey and Jessica, however, were not in the livestock tent.

Then they visited the ring-toss, and the Wheel of Fortune, and the Guess-Your-Weight booth. They whizzed through the United Churches of River Grove cafeteria, past the Crestview High School chorus, and around the Tilt-a-Whirl. They sped past two draft horses pulling three thousand pounds of salt, and the trailer of the Lizard Lady.

Beth looked at her watch. "It's already time to meet Amy," she said mournfully.

"I'll bet she and Sara have got Jeffrey and Jessica with them at the merry-go-round," Matthew said.

But it was just Amy and Sara at the ticket booth. "We didn't find them," Sara said tearfully to her sister. "I'll never complain about being one of five kids again!"

Then Jan and Karen rushed up.

"No luck?" said Amy.

"None," Jan said. "We checked out the Sky Wheel, and the Yo-Yo ride. Nothing."

"Will the Miller family please meet Uncle Walter at the ducking booth?" the loudspeaker boomed.

"The announcer!" said Karen. "That's it! We'll describe Jeffrey and Jessica to him, and someone will turn them in right away!"

"And the winners of the Pretty Baby Contest have been chosen," the loudspeaker thundered on. "Third prize goes to Melissa Wilson. Second prize to Andrew Franks. And first prize to a baby named . . ." There was a long pause. "G.I. Joe?"

"G.I. Joe?!" the Stars squawked.

"The awards are being presented right now, at the stage behind the merry-go-round."

"It has to be Jeffrey!" Beth said grimly. She tore around the carousel.

The Stars and Matthew were just in time to see Jeffrey accepting a large golden trophy. The judge, wearing a top hat, leaned over the blue stroller to tweak Jessica's toes.

"I'm going to kill that kid!" Beth muttered.

"No way!" Amy said as Sara gave Jeffrey a big hug. "Who just won the Pretty Baby Contest? Not the Clovers—the Stars!"

Clovers at the Clubhouse

Thanks to Jeffrey and Jessica, the Stars made it onto the Sesquicentennial video that Wednesday afternoon. On Thursday, their clubhouse was featured in the "Gracious Homes of Old River Grove" tour.

The clubhouse was a small, square building of gray stone, built by J. D. Ellison as a playhouse for his daughter. Sara always said Tiffany Vandermere, the heroine of her novel, would have felt at home there. Beth thought the clubhouse was a pretty special place, too, and it looked fantastic that day.

The geraniums the Stars had planted were blooming in white flowerpots on either side of the door; the green-striped curtains Mrs. Greenfield had made were hanging at the windows; and a blue jay perched on the crooked chimney. The clubhouse was truly beautiful!

The twins and Amy would be hostesses for the first half of the day, Jan and Karen for the second half. Amy was already pacing up and down the walk, fussing and fuming.

"Can you believe I look like such a dork?" she said to Beth and Sara. "Holly probably got her mother's committee to do this dress thing on purpose! I'm just glad the kids at my old school can't see me!"

"I think you look nice," Sara told her. Instead of one of her neon-colored jumpsuits, or a Hard Rock Cafe T-shirt and hand-decorated jeans, Amy was wearing a long, flowered skirt and a long-sleeved white blouse with a high neck. "At least you don't have green hair," Sara added.

"Green hair would make my day," Amy said glumly.

Sara had tied a blue scarf around her head. It matched her long, blue-paisley skirt. Beth's skirt was chocolate brown. They looked related, but not identical.

A stream of visitors poured into the clubhouse soon after the twins arrived. Many of them were older ladies, with lots of questions like "When exactly was this house built?" and "Why is the front door so small?"

The three Stars were just explaining for the umpteenth time how the clubhouse had come to belong to them when Amy hissed, "Red alert! Enemy approaching on the walk!"

The twins peered out a window. Mrs. Hudnut was bearing down on the house, with Holly and Mary Rose Gallagher trotting along behind her.

"They've been dying to see the inside of this place since we got it," Beth said. "Now they can do it legally."

"And they're just in time for the video guys!" Amy pointed toward the road, where the cameraman and his two assistants were unloading their equipment.

"Holly probably tracks them on radar," Sara murmured.

Mrs. Hudnut swept through the front door

and glanced around the one large room. Her gaze locked on the white wicker couch.

"New?" she said to Amy.

"No—actually, it's an antique," Amy replied offhandedly. "Mrs. Ross lent it to us, along with the rocker and the hooked rug. Mrs. Ross gave us the clubhouse, you know."

"Mrs. Ross. . . ." Mrs. Hudnut said thoughtfully. "Really?" Mrs. Ross was born a Topping, as in Topping Park, which was the kind of thing that mattered most to Mrs. Hudnut. She inspected the furniture more closely, while Holly and Mary Rose smirked at the Stars.

"Love your outfit. How does it feel to look like a normal human being?" Holly said casually to Amy.

"Where's Brenda?" Beth interrupted before Amy could explode.

"At the horse show," Holly replied, her nose in the air. "By the time we left, she'd already won two prizes. There'll be a big awards ceremony this afternoon. She'll be videotaped accepting her ribbons, of course."

"Yes, we were videotaped yesterday at the Pretty Baby Contest," Amy announced. "And we're about to be again. . . ."

On cue, the video team knocked at the door. "Are you the owner?" the cameraman asked Mrs. Hudnut, who was checking out the back of the hooked rug.

"No. We are," Beth said firmly, pointing at her sister and Amy.

"Ah! Maybe we could take some footage outside, and then move into the house," he suggested, ushering them out the door.

"Uh . . . I'd rather not be in the video, if you don't mind," Sara mumbled, pulling her scarf farther down on her forehead.

"Oh, don't be silly!" Holly shrieked from the front step. "Your hair goes so well with the green curtains."

"She dyed it that way on purpose to match," Mary Rose added snidely to the cameraman.

Sara's face turned as red as the geraniums. She looked ready to sink into the ground.

"We told you—Sara's hair color is for the River Parade!" Beth said sharply. "And we're going to win so many prizes there won't be room for anyone else on the videotape, period!"

"Girls, I'm finished here," Mrs. Hudnut

broke in as she stepped outside. "Next stop is the Collinsworth mansion. Hurry, hurry!"

"You're going to get a big surprise tomorrow, Holly Hudnut!" Beth was really looking forward to the moment that Holly realized she'd given the Stars their prize-winning theme.

"So are you," Holly warbled as she started down the walk. *"So are you."*

◄ 8 ►

The River Parade

Contestants in the River Parade would launch their boats at Topping Park, then travel downriver to the big parking lot behind Main Street. A reviewing stand had been built there, where the mayor and all the judges would sit. There were also bleachers for the spectators.

The Parade wouldn't start until eleven o'clock, but the Stars were working away by ten, helping Pete and Matthew get the raft set up. For decoration they had Mr. Ellis's stuffed swordfish and Jeffrey's rubber shark, Amanda's inflatable octopus, three coral fans from Karen's shell collection, and an old wooden chest of Mrs.

Bateman's. As a finishing touch, Amy piled the chest high with mounds of her costume jewelry. "Ta-da!" she announced. "Sunken treasure!"

With her greenish hair, and a dark-green fishtail Amy had made from a queen-sized tights leg and a forked piece of cardboard, Sara was the perfect mermaid. A fish, she thought gloomily. When I'm not a twin, I make a great fish.

"Sara, you'll sit near the front of the raft," Amy directed, parading around in tall brown boots, with a silver sword in her belt and a stuffed parrot on her shoulder. "You'll hold the sign, okay?" Karen had painted 20,000 LEAGUES UNDER THE SEA on a worn piece of wood.

"Not bad," said Pete McBride. He was wearing a black eye patch, cut-offs, and a big gold earring.

"Ten more minutes to launching!" a man shouted through a bullhorn.

"I think it looks great!" Beth exclaimed, stepping back to admire the raft. She was wearing jeans with jagged bottoms, a striped T-shirt, and a big satin sash.

"Can you see Holly and the Clovers?" Sara

asked from her place on the raft. With her fishtail on, she couldn't stand up. In fact, she could hardly move at all.

Jan shook her head. "There are too many boats." Within a few feet of "20,000 Leagues" there was a Viking ship, a Hawaiian war canoe, an old car on floats, and a rowboat decorated to look like a giant lobster.

"Five more minutes!" the man yelled through the bullhorn.

"Let's do it!" said Matthew, who was wearing a fake mustache and a black-felt pirate hat with a white skull and crossbones on the front. "Who's in the wheel first?"

"I am," said Pete, taking his place inside it and hanging on to the rod through the center.

"Start handing me the water balloons," Matthew said to Beth and Amy. He and Pete had filled over two hundred of them the night before, and piled them into the trunk of Mrs. Ellis's car. Soon there was a huge mound of grapefruit-sized balloons on the raft, next to the V-shaped balloon launcher.

Amy and Jan would use two paddles to steer the boat, Karen would feed water balloons to Matthew, and Beth would take a turn in the wheel when Pete got tired.

"Ready, everybody?" the man with the bullhorn hollered.

"Ready!" the River Paraders roared.

"The River Parade has officially begun. *Bon voyage!*"

Things were pretty crowded in the beginning, when all the boats and rafts were being launched. After a few minutes, however, the crowd began to thin out. The faster boats shot ahead, and the slower ones lagged behind. That's when the crew of "20,000 Leagues" spotted their primary target.

"Clone-ers off the starboard bow!" Matthew sang out. "Whatever that means."

"Have you ever seen anything prissier?" Amy exclaimed, disgusted.

Holly and the Clovers were perched on an old bicycle frame with five seats that was mounted on a raft. They were wearing matching straw hats, starched white middy blouses, long blue skirts, white stockings, and high-topped shoes. Their sign read, BICYCLE BUILT FOR FIVE, and a tape deck was blaring out an ancient song—". . . a bicycle built for twoooooo."

"Let's drench 'em!" Beth said, glowering like a bloodthirsty pirate.

"They're really moving along," said Jan.

The Clovers' pedaling was what pushed their raft forward. As soon as they noticed the Stars, they pedaled like crazy.

"Faster, Pete. Faster!" Amy urged.

"I'm running as fast as I can!" Pete puffed from inside the wheel.

"No sweat," said Matthew, taking the water balloon Karen handed him. "We'll blitz them long-distance."

He pulled back on the pieces of inner tube, positioned the balloon on the square of canvas in the center, aimed, and let fly.

"Too far to the right," Amy said as the balloon hit the water with a splash. It missed the Clovers by several feet.

Matthew launched another one.

"Too far to the left," Beth told him.

"I've got 'em now!" Matthew chuckled and launched the third balloon. . . . *Splat!* Bull's-eye on Brenda Wallace!

The Clovers pedaled harder, but Matthew managed to hit Sue Pinson, and finally Holly, drenching her straw hat with its blue ribbons. The Stars could hear Holly shriek angrily over all the noise of the other River Paraders.

"They're slowing down!" Amy said.

"We'll get really close!"

Pete's legs churned, and Matthew sent balloon after balloon sailing into the air toward the Clovers. Soon the 20,000 Leaguers were so close they could *throw* the water balloons. The Clovers' blouses and skirts were dripping, their straw hats wilting over their faces. Their raft was dead in the water.

Then, when there was only a yard or so of river separating the two groups, Holly Hudnut leaned down and picked up what looked like a piece of thick black rope.

"I think it's a hose!" Karen exclaimed.

"Pedal!" Holly screeched to her troops.

The Clovers pedaled furiously, but they couldn't make their raft move. Holly pointed the black hose at the Stars. Before they had time to think, river water shot through the hose as if it were a cannon. In seconds, everybody on the "20,000 Leagues" raft was soaked to the skin.

"Surprise!" said Holly through gritted teeth.

◀ 9 ▶
Mayor for a Day

"I can't believe it!" Matthew Ellis said. "We actually have to share a crummy trophy with the Clone-ers!"

By the time the Stars, Matthew, Pete, and the Clovers had reached the reviewing stand, they didn't stand a chance of winning the grand prize. They were all too wet for the judges to be able to tell *what* their costumes were supposed to look like. But there were smaller prizes, and the one for Most Unusual Power Source was split between the Stars' raft and the Clovers'.

Amy pulled out her soaking-wet lists. "So it's Stars 2½, Clovers 2½."

"And the Clovers probably deserve at least

half a point for that water cannon of theirs," Karen told her.

"The grand prize," Mayor Watkins announced from the reviewing stand, "goes to the Viking ship, manned by the Svenson family."

Mr. Svenson climbed the ladder from the river to the parking lot to pick up his trophy to great applause.

"There go gift certificates for two-hundred-dollars' worth of albums, two ten-speeds, and a year's worth of movie passes," Matthew said gloomily.

"Let's get this thing out of the water," said Pete.

Richie had driven the Batemans' truck to the finish line. He was waiting to haul the raft out when the mayor spoke again. "I'd like to take this opportunity to make another important announcement. The winner of the elementary schools' Mayor-for-a-Day Contest has been chosen. . . ."

The Stars were barely listening, since they were helping Richie attach a line to the raft.

The mayor went on, "And that winner is . . . Miss Sara Greenfield!"

"Wha-at?!" Amy yelled. "Way to go, Sara!"

"Down with the Clovers!" shouted Pete and Matthew.

"Sara, you won!" Beth and Jan shrieked, jumping up and down.

"Let's try not to tip the raft over," Karen warned nervously. "Congrats, Sara—that's wonderful!"

"A fish for mayor?" Holly Hudnut yelled loudly from the Clovers' raft.

For once, Sara didn't pay any attention. She was too flabbergasted to care what Holly said.

"Miss Greenfield has written a beautiful composition about what River Grove means to her, called 'Friends and Family,' " Mayor Watkins was saying. "It will be printed in the Sunday Sesquicentennial edition of the *River Grove Courier*. A copy of it will also be included in the time capsule. Now, Sara, if you'll just climb up here, I have a medal to present to you."

"I can't move," Sara whispered frantically to her sister. Both of her legs were stuffed into the fishtail Amy had made.

"Take the tail off," Amy said. "You've got your bathing suit on underneath."

"I can't get undressed with the whole town watching me!" Sara croaked.

The mayor was waiting expectantly on the bulkhead above the river.

"I'll go for you," Beth said quickly. "Twins are good for *something*." She ran up the ladder in her pirate outfit and shook Mayor Watkins' hand.

"Sara Greenfield?" he asked.

"That's right," said Beth. "And thank you very much for the award."

"Congratulations. You're a very talented girl," Mayor Watkins said warmly. "As Mayor for the Day, you'll be riding in the lead car tomorrow for the March up Main Street."

As the Stars squealed excitedly from their raft on the river, a very wet Holly Hudnut stormed across the parking lot, climbed into her mother's car, and slammed the door shut.

"And since your composition makes it clear how much your friends mean to you"— the mayor smiled down at the Stars on the raft—"perhaps you'd like to have them ride with you."

"That would be terrific!" said Beth. She

made a thumbs-up sign to her sister. If Sara has any doubts about what she can do for the Stars—any doubts about herself at all, Beth was thinking, then she is crazy!

• • •

At noon the next day, Sara Greenfield was perched on the back of a bright-yellow Cadillac convertible. Beth and Karen and Jan were sitting in the backseat with her, and Amy was in the front seat next to the driver. The Crestview High School band blared out the first notes of the Grand March, and the yellow Cadillac rolled slowly forward up Main Street. Sunlight gleamed on Sara's greenish-red hair as she waved to the crowds. The funniest thing, she was thinking to herself, is that I don't have stage fright, no stage fright at all. And she blew a kiss to Holly and the Clovers, who were scowling on the front steps of Mr. Hudnut's bank.